GHETTO PHILOSOPHY
by
DE VITA M. LEDGISTER

Absolutely mind stimulating encouraging words from one spirit to another…M.H., Sacramento, Calif.

Thought provoking monuments that will stand the test of time….T.D.R., Somerdale, New Jersey

The kind of words that make you think before you react….S.H. ,Philadelphia, PA.

Character building, integrity based sayings that have been handed down from generations of the past..…S.H., Anchorage, Alaska

The art of mindful thought placed into verbal perspective within a literary context…N.H.C., Orlando, Florida

"Ghetto Philosophy". Wisdom and/or advice from various perspectives to encourage others to follow the right path….H.L.R., Dallas, Texas

GHETTO PHILOSOPHY

By: DeVita M. Ledgister

Ghetto Philosophy
By: DeVita M. Ledgister

Cover design by: DeVita M. Ledgister
Logo design by: Andre M. Saunders
Editor: Anelda L. Ballard
Templates by: DeVita M. Ledgister:
Photography by: Brian Kerner

© 2010 Ghetto Philosophy
ISBN 978-0-9843255-4-2
ISBN 0-9843255-4-9
Library of Congress Control Number: 2009944148

All rights reserved. This book is protected under the copyright laws of the United States of America. This book may not be copied or reprinted for commercial gain or profit. The use of short quotations or occasional page copying for personal or group study is permitted and encouraged. Permission will be granted upon request.

For Worldwide Distribution. Printed in the United States of America.
Published by Jazzy Kitty Greetings Marketing & Publishing, LLC.
Utilizing Microsoft Publishing Software.

ACKNOWLEDGMENTS

To my Mom, Dad, God Mother, Aunts, Uncles, older brother, younger sister, all my cousins, and neighborhood mentors….just when you thought I wasn't listening, I was. When others had movie stars and sports figures to look up to as role models, I was blessed with all of you. Never can I ever remember a time when I asked for anything from any of you that I was denied. Lucky me. I love you.

To my academic and mostly to my spiritual teachers, thank you for helping me to understand that giving up is never an option. Thank you for helping me not to just know that I have an inheritance, but to also understand why **THE INHERITANCE** is truly mine.

Tiffany, L.J., Tray, Mathew and J.D., you will have a lot of new beginnings throughout life. Please remain mindful that each one is a new journey, a new adventure and a great blessing. I love you.

To my Prayer Line family, thank you for being there each and every morning at 6:00 am to praise God with me, to pray me through my day, and to help me get dressed in my spiritual armor.

Haston (Pancho) Thornton, Dwight Jackson, Rick Johnson, and Joey Bey, thank you all for being life long friends, encouraging me, listening to my outlandish ideas, laughing with me/at me and helping me to wipe away the tears.

DEDICATIONS

To my Mom, Dad and all my Family, both immediate and extended. I love you and always will.

TABLE OF CONTENTS

Introduction.. i

Things That Begin to be Cheap.. 01

If It Wasn't for Book Smart People..................................... 02

Even If One of the Best.. 03

Round Tables... 04

You're Not a Real Man.. 05

Every Smiling Face... 06

Success Doesn't Mean a Thing... 07

Don't Walk Faster Than Your Feet....................................... 08

April Showers.. 09

Just Because It's a Black Thought...................................... 10

Women are the Closest Thing to a Man's Death........................... 11

The Wise... 12

Jail Make You Miss a Person.. 13

A Man Can Love a Women... 14

Oh, You Want Me to Love You 15

Women, You Can't Live With Them.. 16

Your Body Turns.. 17

Lay Down with Dogs... 18

I Stopped Worrying About People.. 19

Money Can Buy Love... 20

Rome Wasn't Built in a Day... 21

Think Long... 22

TABLE OF CONTENTS

It's Not What You are That Counts.............................. 23
What Goes Around.. 24
Three Minutes of Pleasure.................................. 25
What is a Kiss???... 26
Efforts are Meaningless...................................... 27
Sometimes You Have to Put Your Hand Over
Your Mouth.. 28
I Cried Because.. 29
Let the Door Hit You.. 30
If You Can't Stand the Heat................................ 31
If the Shoe Fits.. 32
Lord Don't Come.. 33
God Don't Like... 34
A Drunk Man 35
Men are Like Buses.. 36
Cry Poor.. 37
Birds of a Feather... 38
A Stray Bullet.. 39
One Bad Apple.. 40
You Can Take the Horse to the Water................ 41
It's Easy to Get into the System.......................... 42
Everybody wants to Go to Heaven..................... 43
Sometimes You Have to Steal from Peter.......... 44

TABLE OF CONTENTS

Notice…Wash Your Hands…… 45
Men Drink When They Are Stressed…… 46
Beauty is Only Skin Deep, But…… 47
Nothing Beats a Failure But…… 48
Never Judge a Book By…… 49
Don't No One Monkey Stop…… 50
If It Looks Like A Duck…… 51
If You Ever Want to Hide Something…… 52
61 Years of Marriage…… 53
Do It…… 54
Somethings …… 55
Just Because You're Loud…… 56
Put That in Your Pipe and Smoke It…… 57
The First Horse Out the Stall…… 58
Little Streams…… 59
You Get More with Honey…… 60
Everybody Is Nice…… 61
If You're Looking to Get to the Top…… 62
Is That the Pot…… 63
Fake It 'Til…… 64
About the Author…… 65

INTRODUCTION

"Ghetto Philosophy" has been a work in progress since the early times of my youth. During many occasions in my younger life, when I was just sitting around the house or yard listening to my grandfather and uncles as they played cards while drinking their Southern Comfort with the heavy stench of Camel cigarettes, I can remember the conversations and the sayings that went along with the moment. Momma, my grandmother, would comment day after day with proverbial sayings in order to get her point across. Dad, with his Jamaican bloodline, made it a point to correct and discipline myself and my siblings with thoughtful and mindful commentaries that made one think deeper than either one of us wanted to endure.

As time endeared and the years progressed, watching the neighborhood chess, checker and serious card games around the neighborhood park, one surely would hear colorful thoughts so artfully expressed with words of wisdom, teaching the younger generation about life.

Within the passing of two to three generations during my time, I am glad to share some of the thoughts and sayings that may not have trickled down from past generations. Those of you who read this small memento, please be mindful that this too is a link into past cultural history that may, and can be useful for the future.

THINGS THAT BEGIN TO BE CHEAP...

Things that begin to be cheap can end up being an expensive habit.

IF IT WASN'T FOR BOOK SMART PEOPLE...

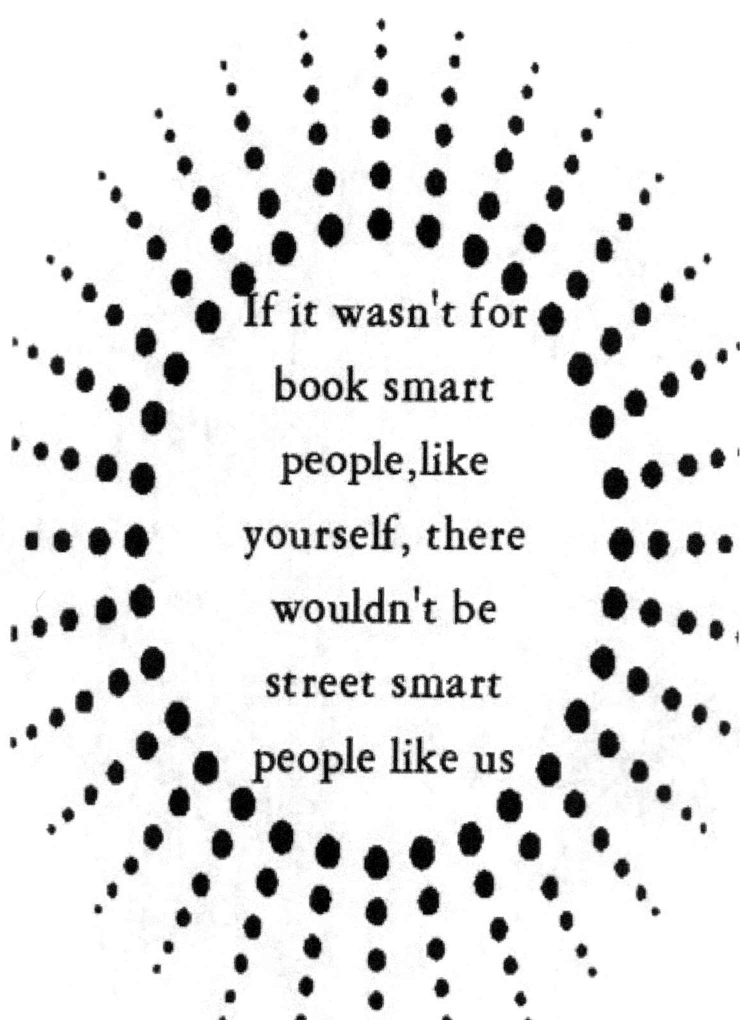
If it wasn't for
book smart
people,like
yourself, there
wouldn't be
street smart
people like us

EVEN IF ONE OF THE BEST...

Even if one of the best writers, producers or directors of a movie die in the middle of the movie, that doesn't mean that the movie is over.

ROUND TABLES...

Round tables
always mean
you have to
hear a bunch
of rhetoric

YOU'RE NOT A REAL MAN...

You're not a real
man if you've
never been to jail,
but you're a
better man if you
haven't.

EVERY SMILING FACE...

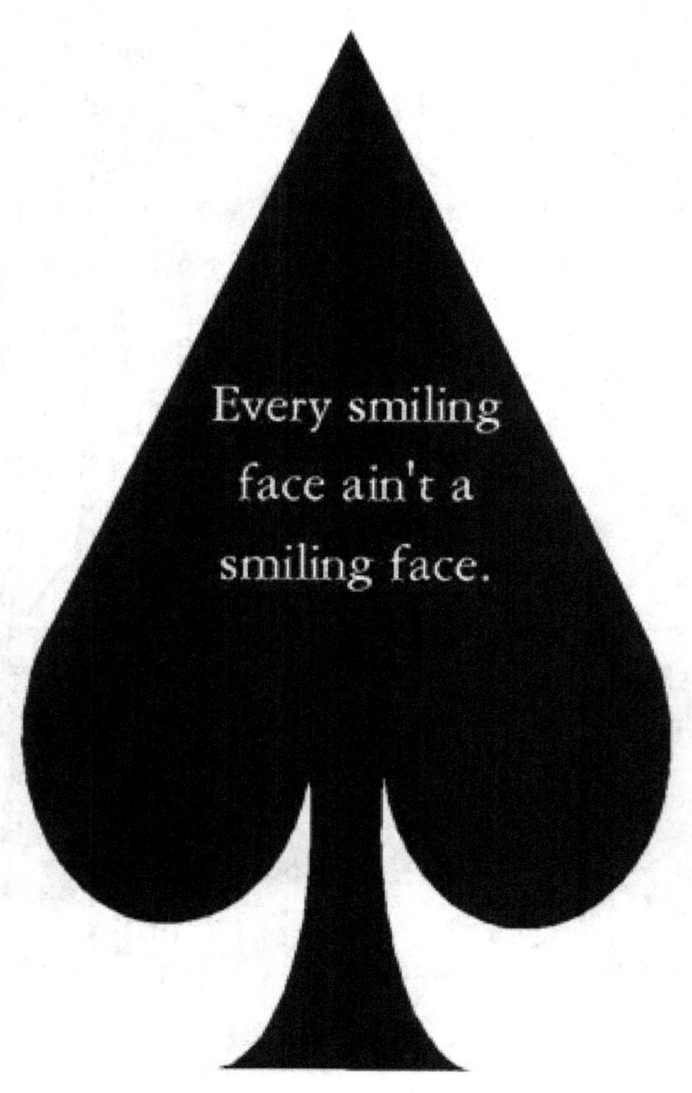
Every smiling
face ain't a
smiling face.

SUCCESS DOESN'T MEAN A THING...

Success doesn't mean a
thing if you don't have
anyone to share it with.

DON'T WALK FASTER THAN YOUR FEET CAN GO...

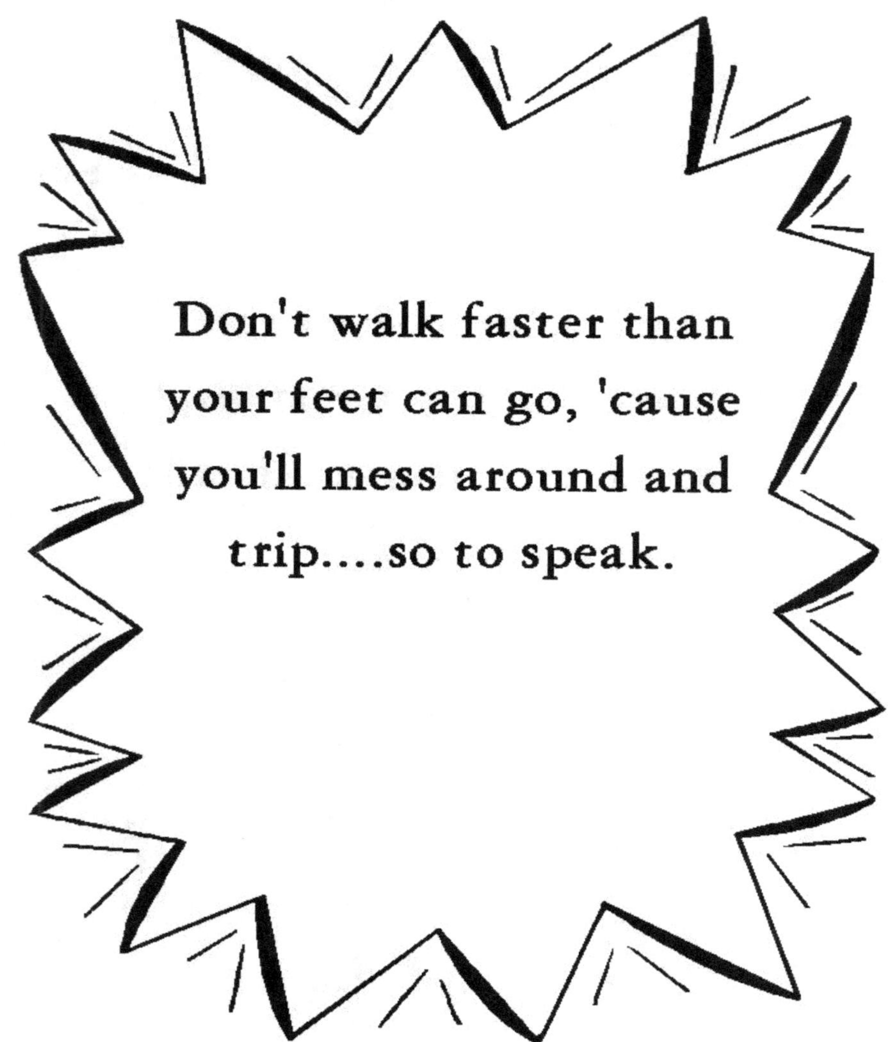
Don't walk faster than
your feet can go, 'cause
you'll mess around and
trip....so to speak.

APRIL SHOWERS...

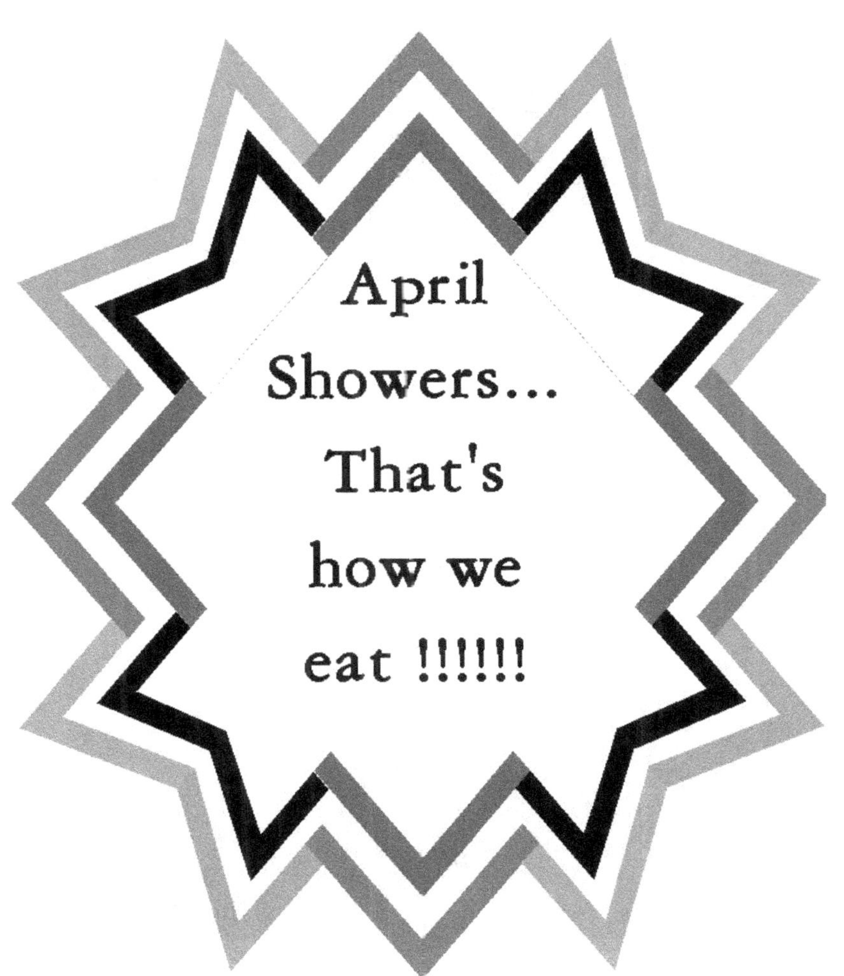
April
Showers...
That's
how we
eat !!!!!!

JUST BECAUSE IT'S A BLACK THOUGHT...

Just because it's a Black thought doesn't mean White people can't read it.

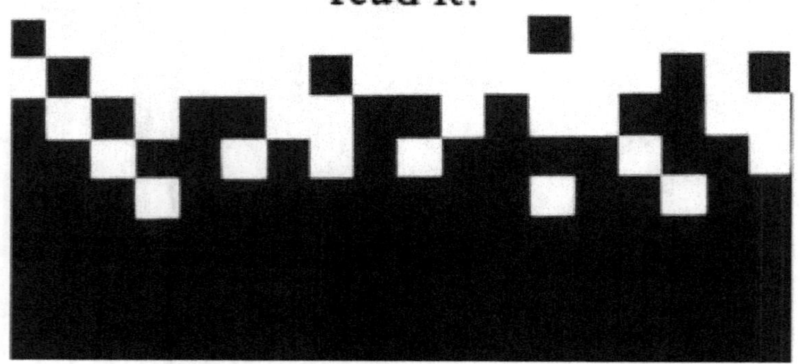

WOMEN ARE THE CLOSEST THING TO A MAN'S DEATH...

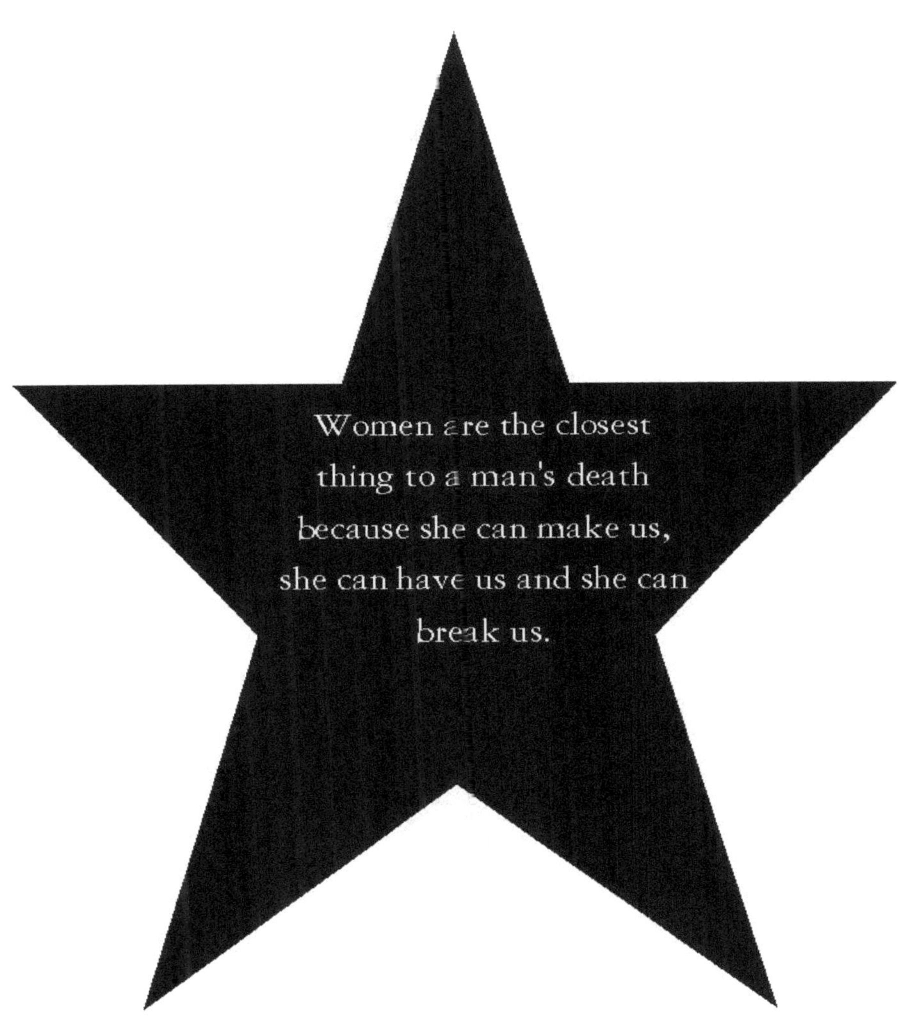
Women are the closest
thing to a man's death
because she can make us,
she can have us and she can
break us.

THE WISE...

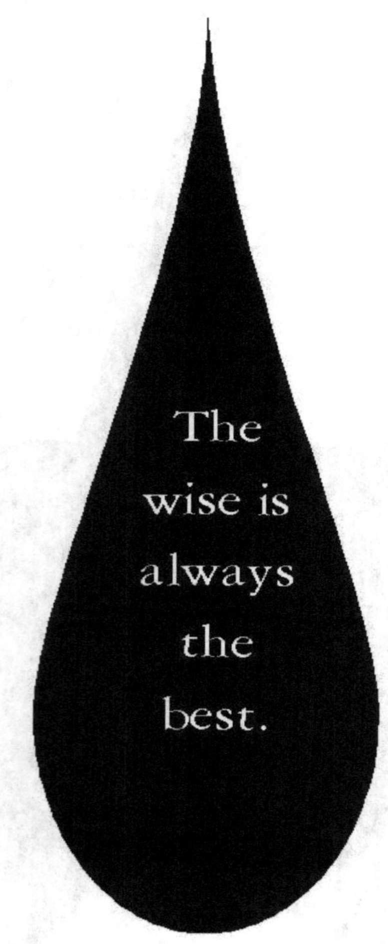
The
wise is
always
the
best.

JAIL MAKES YOU MISS A PERSON...

Jail makes you miss a person harder and longer and deeper because you can't have them when you want to.....almost like death.

A MAN CAN LOVE A WOMEN...

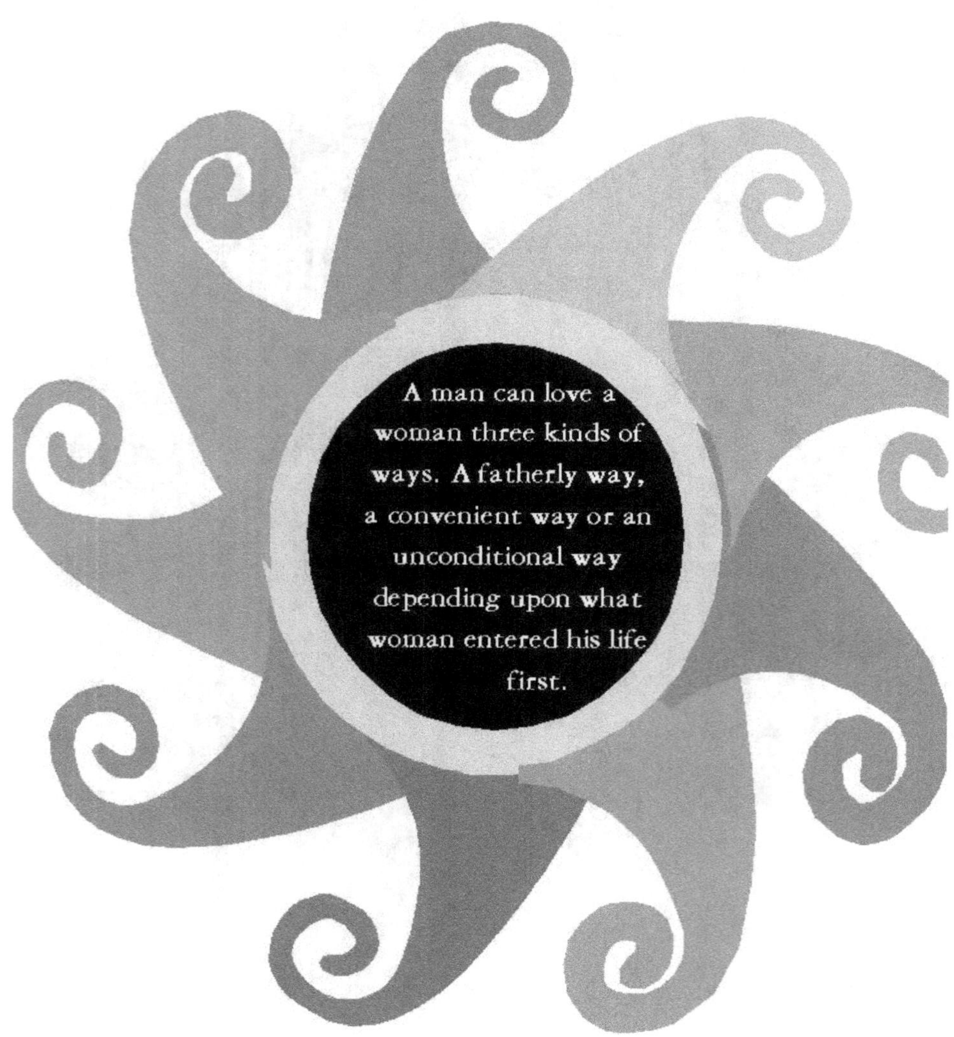
A man can love a
woman three kinds of
ways. A fatherly way,
a convenient way or an
unconditional way
depending upon what
woman entered his life
first.

OH, YOU WANT ME TO LOVE YOU...

Oh, you want me to
love you the way you
would love you if I
were you.........

WOMEN, YOU CAN'T LIVE WITH THEM...

Women, you can't live with them, and you can't kill them.

YOUR BODY TURNS...

Your body turns in the direction your mind is facing.

LAY DOWN WITH DOGS...

Lay down
with
dogs.......
you'll wake
up with fleas

I STOPPED WORRYING ABOUT PEOPLE LIKING ME...

I STOPPED WORRYING ABOUT PEOPLE LIKING ME WHEN I FINALLY REALIZED THAT THE ONLY ONE WHO NEEDS TO SHOW UP AT MY FUNERAL WAS ME.

MONEY CAN BUY...

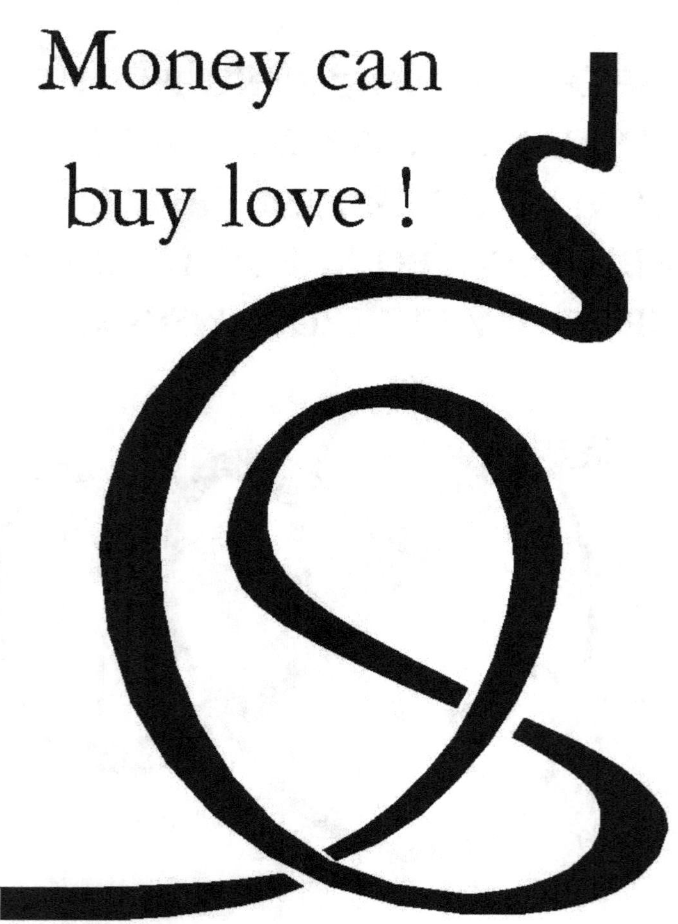
Money can
buy love !

ROME WASN'T BUILT IN A DAY...

Rome wasn't
built in a day,
but on a daily
basis.

THINK LONG...

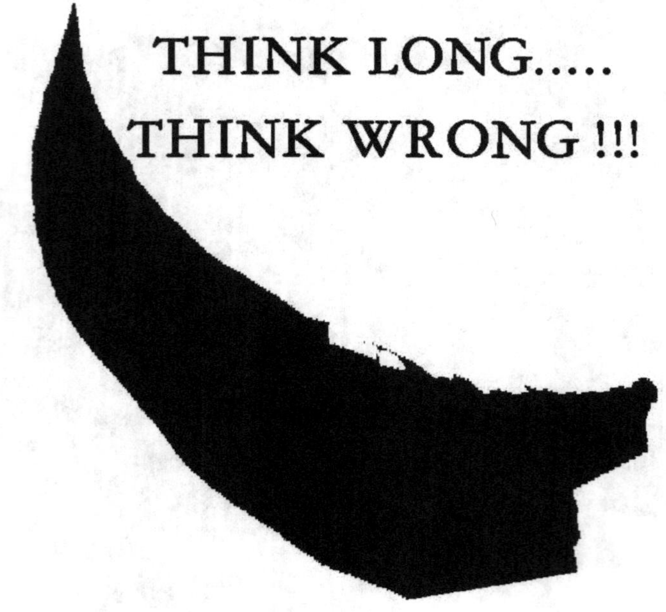
THINK LONG.....
THINK WRONG !!!

IT'S NOT WHAT YOU ARE THAT COUNTS...

IT'S NOT WHAT YOU
ARE THAT COUNTS;
IT'S WHAT PEOPLE
THINK YOU ARE.

WHAT GOES AROUND...

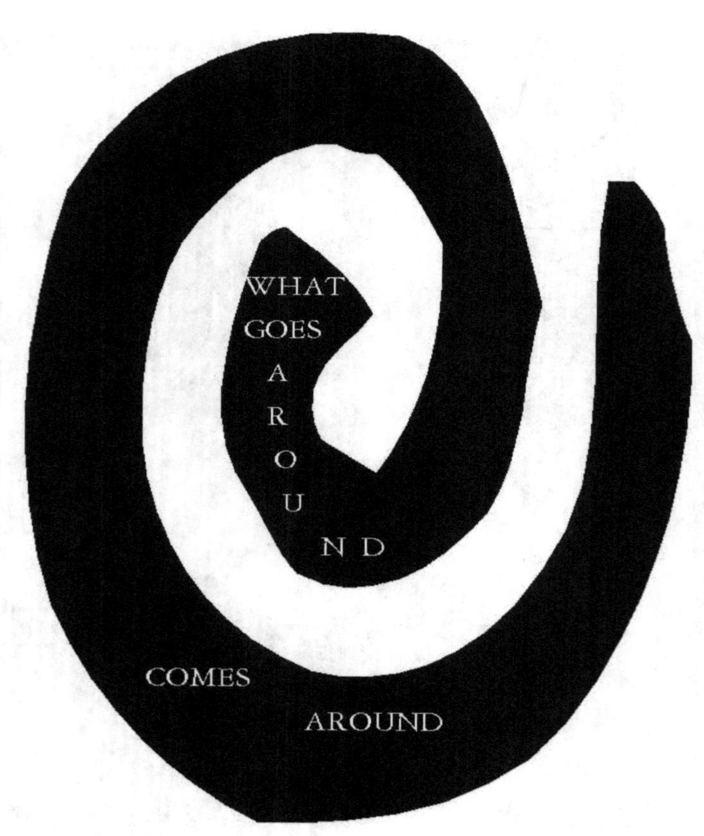
WHAT
GOES
A
R
O
U
N D
COMES
AROUND

THREE MINUTES OF PLEASURE...

THREE MINUTES
OF PLEASURE
ISN'T WORTH
THIRTY YEARS
OF CRAZINESS
!!!!!!

WHAT IS A KISS?????

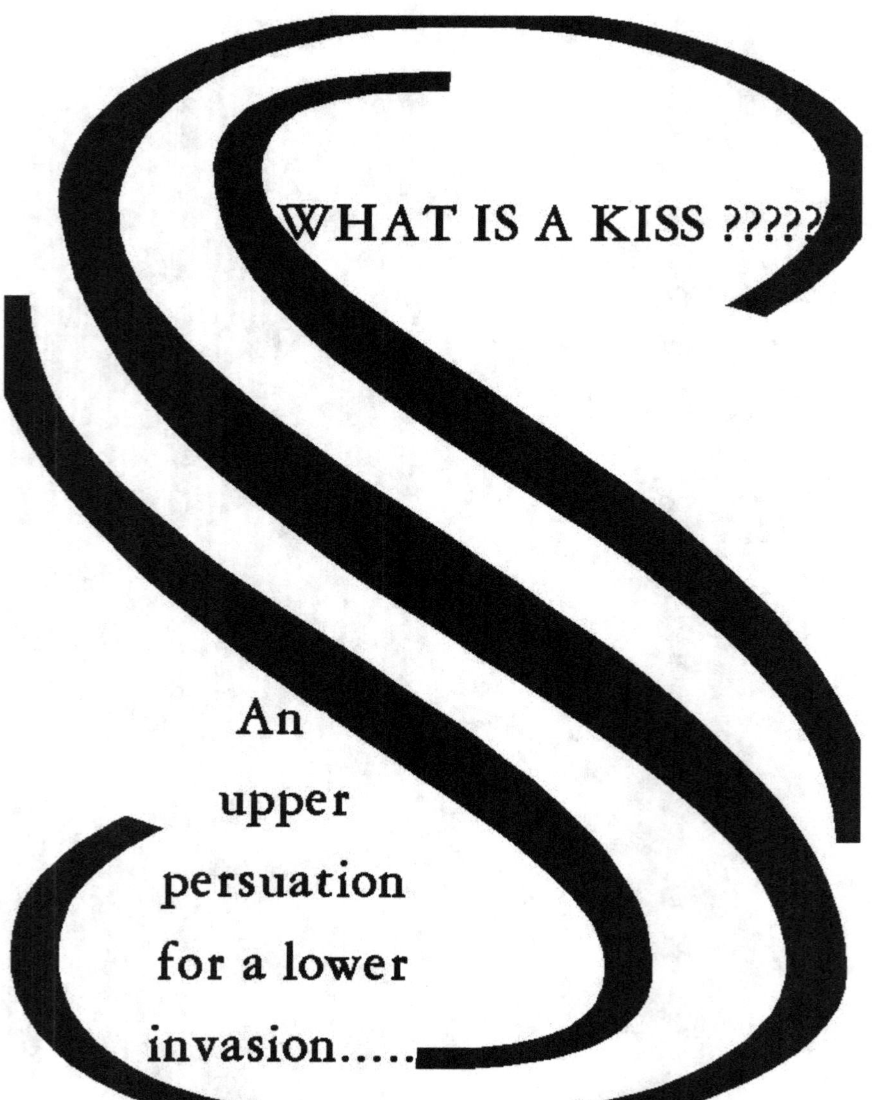
WHAT IS A KISS ?????
An
upper
persuation
for a lower
invasion.....

EFFORTS ARE MEANINGLESS...

****
EFFORTS ARE
MEANINGLESS
****
RESULTS ARE
EVERYTHING
****

SOMETIMES YOU HAVE TO PUT YOUR HAND OVER YOUR MOUTH IF...

SOMETIMES YOU HAVE
TO PUT YOUR HAND
OVER YOUR MOUTH IF
YOU CAN'T STOP
TALKING....!!!!!

I CRIED BECAUSE...

I cried because I
didn't have a new
pair of shoes until
I saw a man with
no feet.

LET THE DOOR HIT YOU...

Let the door hit you where the good Lord split you.

IF YOU CAN'T STAND THE HEAT...

If you can't stand
the heat....
GET OUT OF THE
KITCHEN !!!!!!

IF

THE SHOE

FITS,

WEAR IT

!!!!!!!

LORD DON'T COME...

Lord don't come
when you want
Him, but He sure
is always on time.

GOD DON'T LIKE...

GOD
DON'T
LIKE
UGLY!

A DRUNK MAN...

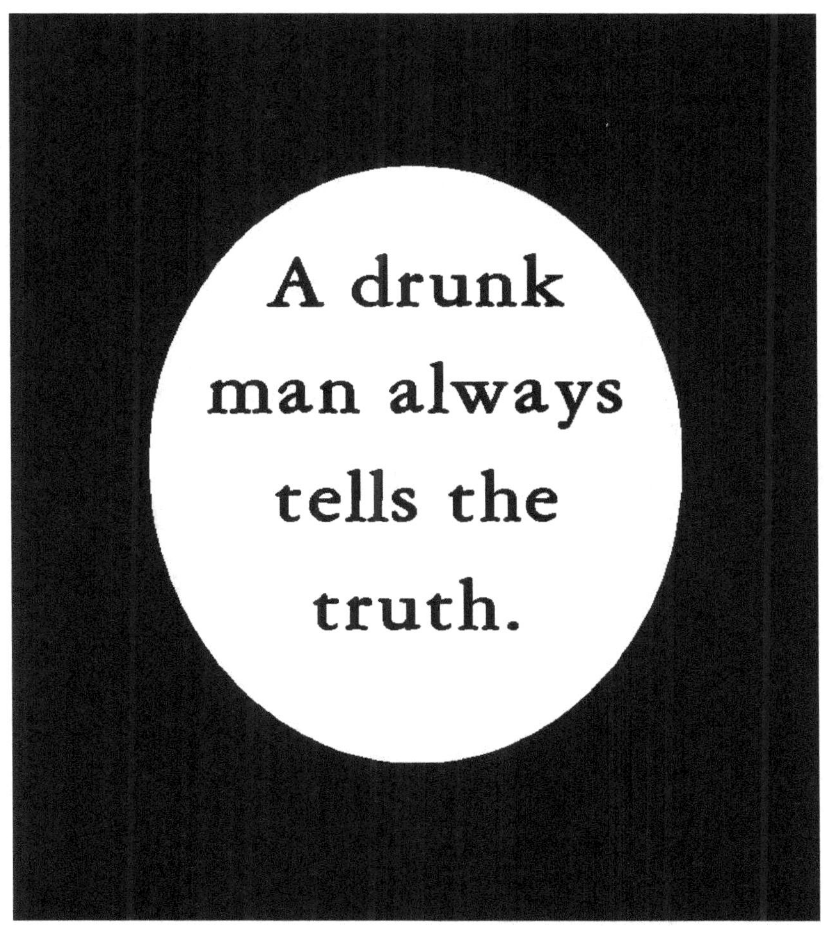
A drunk
man always
tells the
truth.

MEN ARE LIKE BUSES...

Men are like
buses, never
run after one
because
there's
always
another one
coming.

CRY POOR...

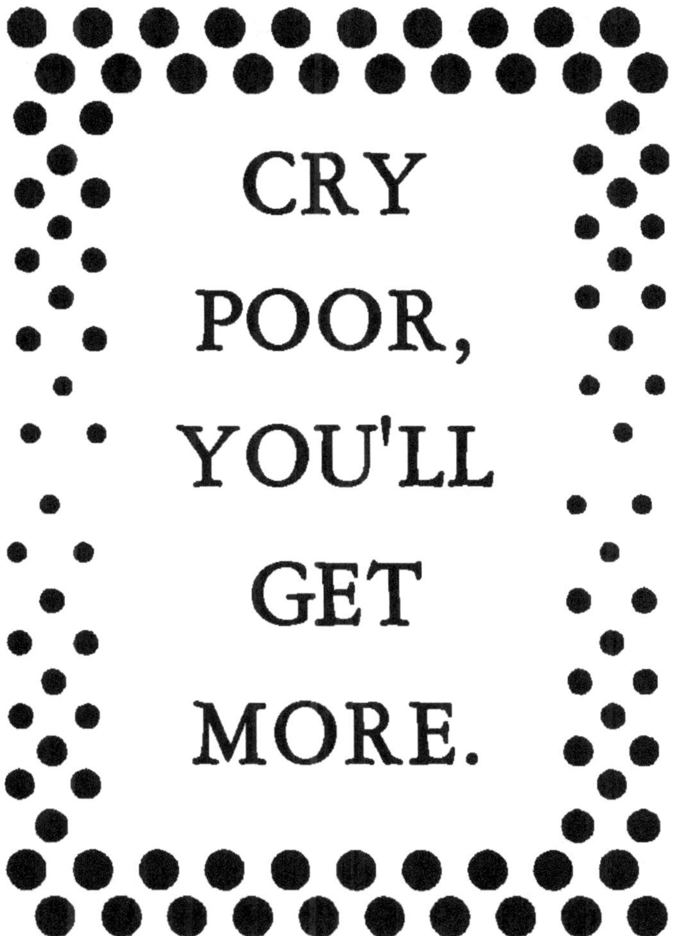
CRY
POOR,
YOU'LL
GET
MORE.

BIRDS OF A FEATHER...

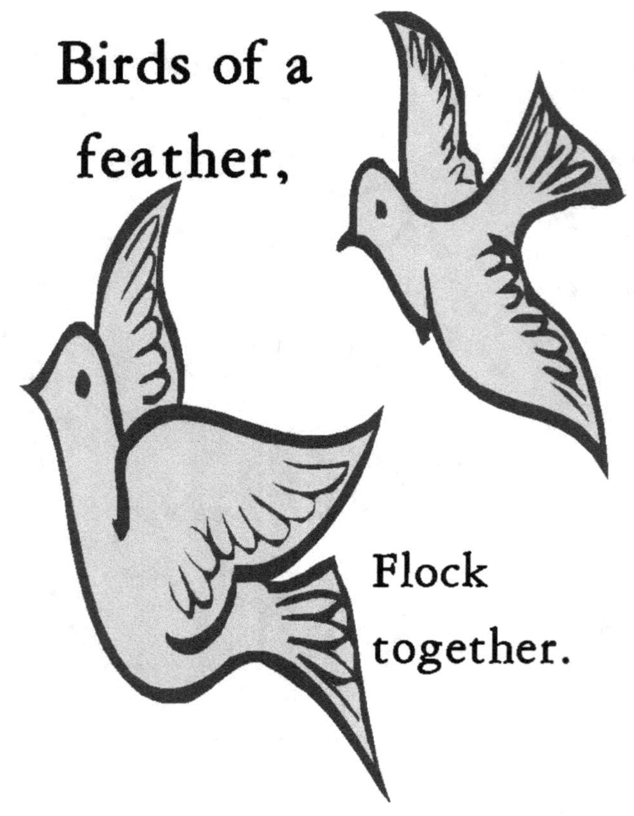
Birds of a
feather,
Flock
together.

A STRAY BULLET...

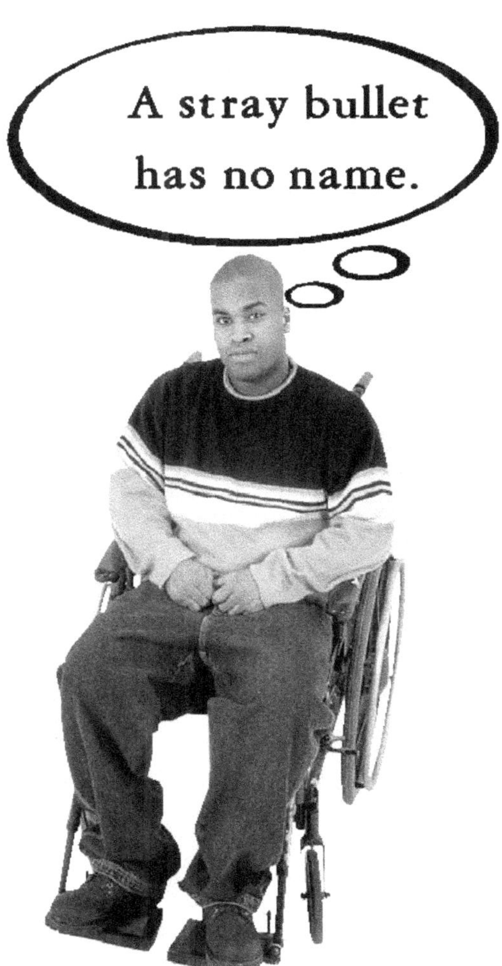
A stray bullet
has no name.

ONE BAD APPLE...

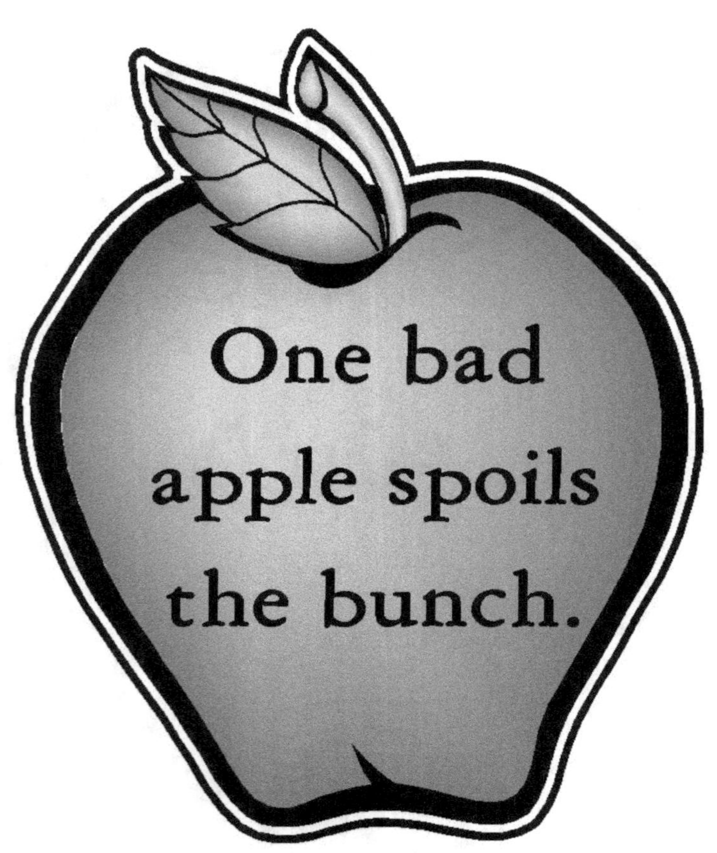
One bad
apple spoils
the bunch.

YOU CAN TAKE THE HORSE TO THE WATER...

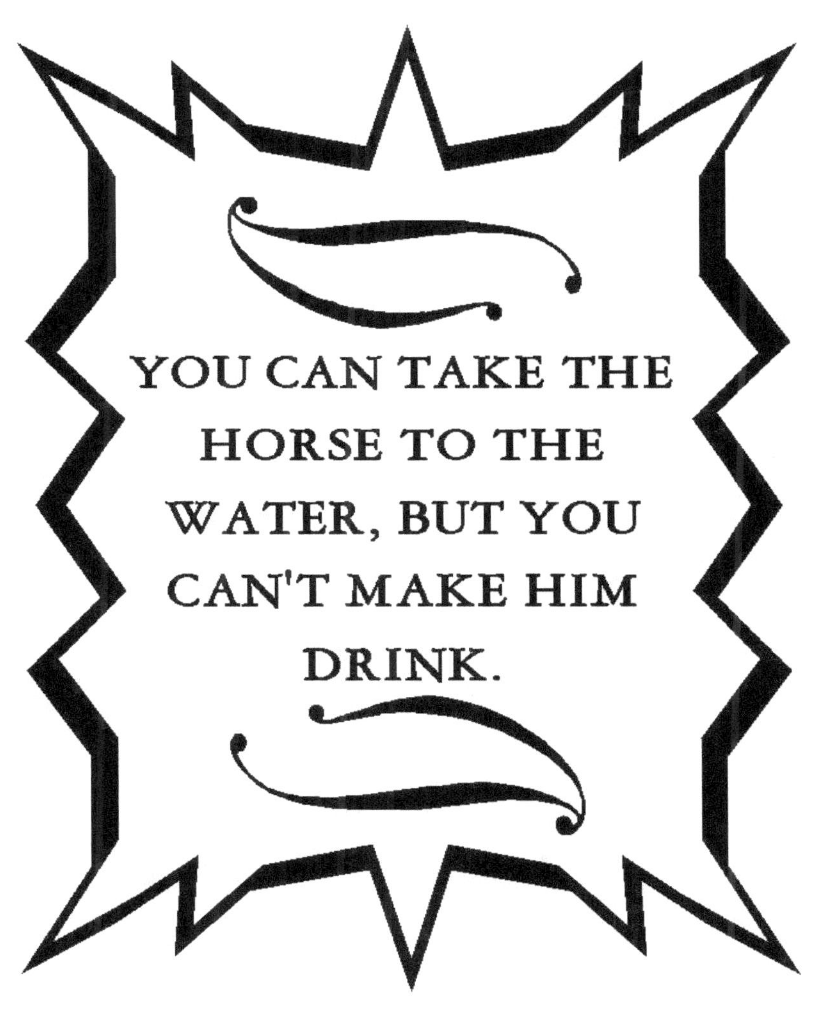
YOU CAN TAKE THE
HORSE TO THE
WATER, BUT YOU
CAN'T MAKE HIM
DRINK.

IT'S EASY TO GET INTO THE SYSTEM...

IT'S EASY TO GET
INTO THE SYSTEM
AND HARD AS HELL
TO GET OUT!!!

EVERYBODY WANTS TO GO TO HEAVEN BUT...

Everybody wants
to go to heaven,
but nobody wants
to die to get
there.

SOMETIMES YOU HAVE TO STEAL FROM PETER...

SOMETIMES YOU HAVE TO STEAL FROM PETER IN ORDER TO PAY PAUL.

NOTICE...WASH YOUR HANDS

NOTICE
Wash Your
Hands

CLEANLINESS IS NEXT TO GODLINESS

MEN DRINK WHEN THEY ARE STRESSED...

Men drink when they are stressed;
Women eat when they are stressed.

BEAUTY IS ONLY SKIN DEEP, BUT...

BEAUTY IS
ONLY SKIN
DEEP, BUT
UGLINESS IS TO
THE BONE.

NOTHING BEATS A FAILURE BUT...

Nothing
beats a
failure but
a try.

NEVER JUDGE A BOOK BY...

NEVER
JUDGE A
BOOK BY
IT'S
COVER

DON'T NO ONE MONKEY STOP...

DON'T NO
ONE
MONKEY
STOP NO
SHO'

IF IT LOOKS LIKE A DUCK...

If it looks like a duck, walks like a
duck, sounds like a duck.....then
it's a DUCK !!!!!!!
?

IF YOU EVER WANT TO HIDE SOMETHING...

If you ever want to hide something...put it inside a book.

61 **YEARS OF MARRIARGE...**

61years of marriage..It wasn't always a bed of roses, but we made it !

DO IT...

Do it. Do it right the first time and never have to do it again.

SOMETHINGS...

Somethings are not left up to one individual.

JUST BECAUSE YOU'RE LOUD...

JUST
because
you're loud
doesn't make
you right !

PUT THAT IN YOUR PIPE...

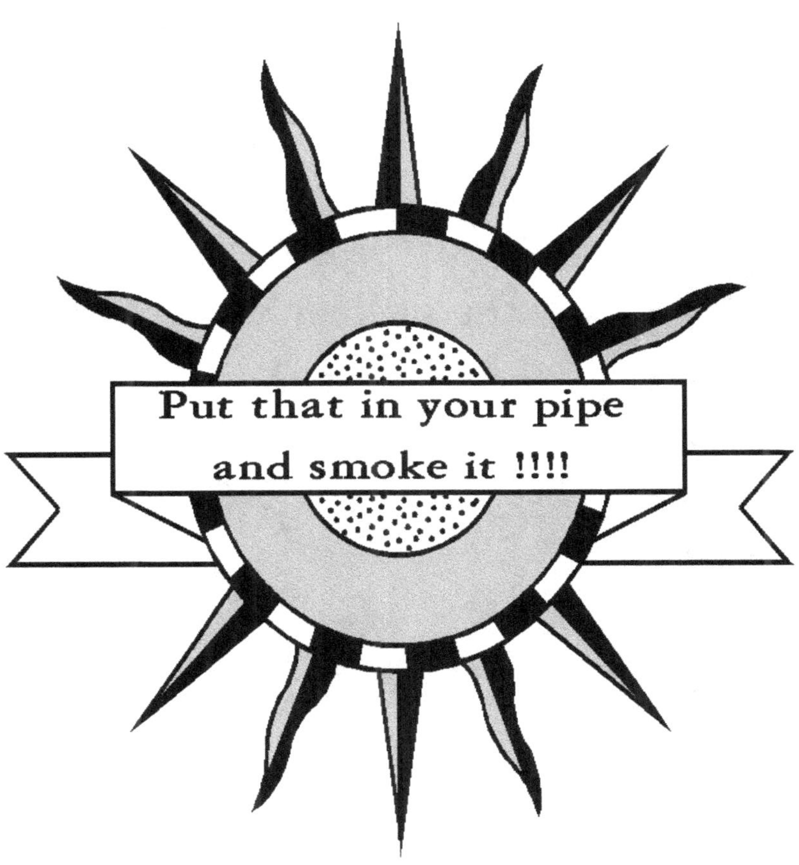
Put that in your pipe
and smoke it !!!!

THE FIRST HORSE OUT THE STALL...

The first horse out
the stall ain't
necessarily the
winner.

LITTLE STREAMS...

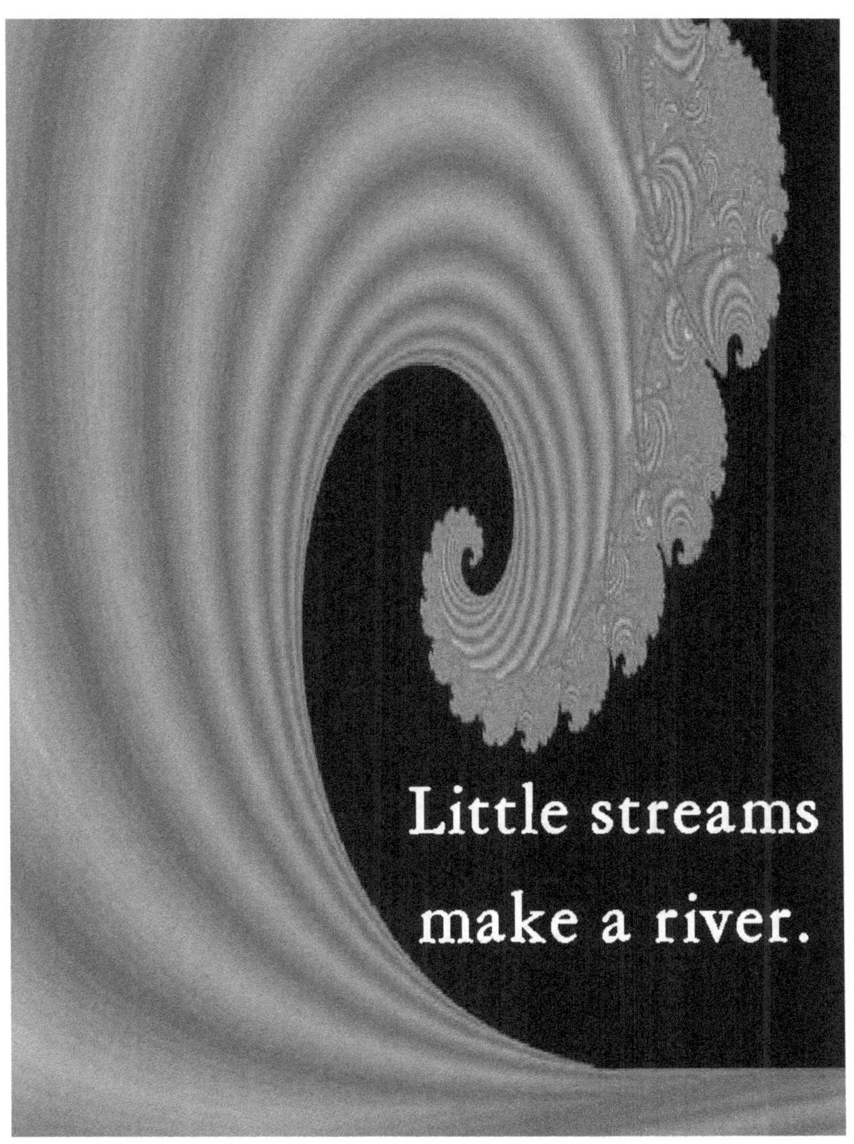
Little streams
make a river.

YOU GET MORE BEES WITH HONEY...

You get more bees with
honey than you do with
vinegar.

EVERYBODY IS NICE...

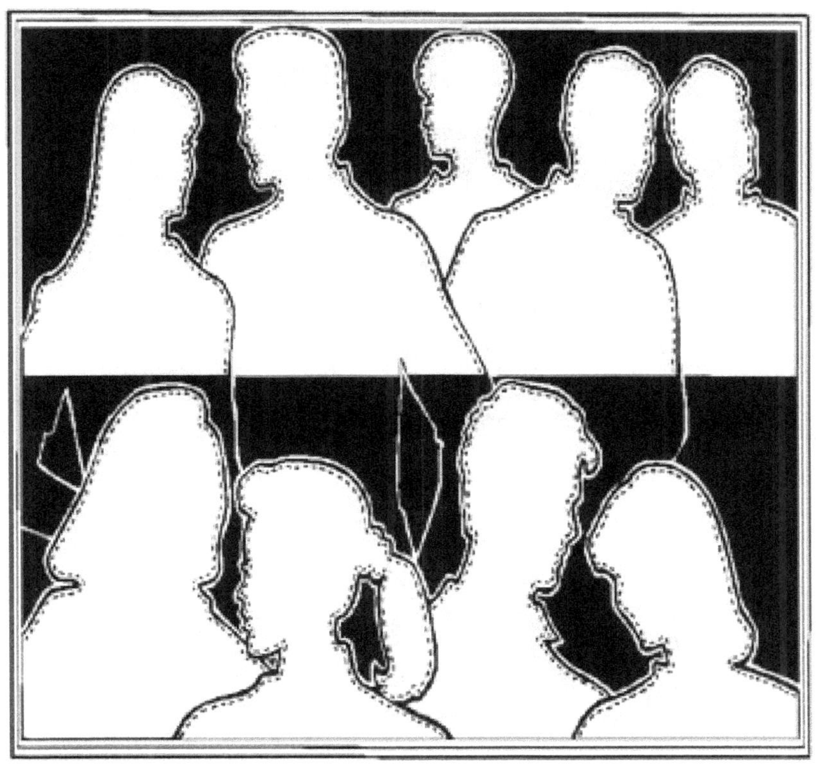

EVERYBODY IS NICE ....IN THE BEGINNING.

IF YOU'RE LOOKING TO GET TO THE TOP...

If you're looking to get to the top....you may get there quicker if you would stop complaining and start doin'.

IS THAT THE POT...

Is that the pot calling the kettle black ????

FAKE IT 'TIL...

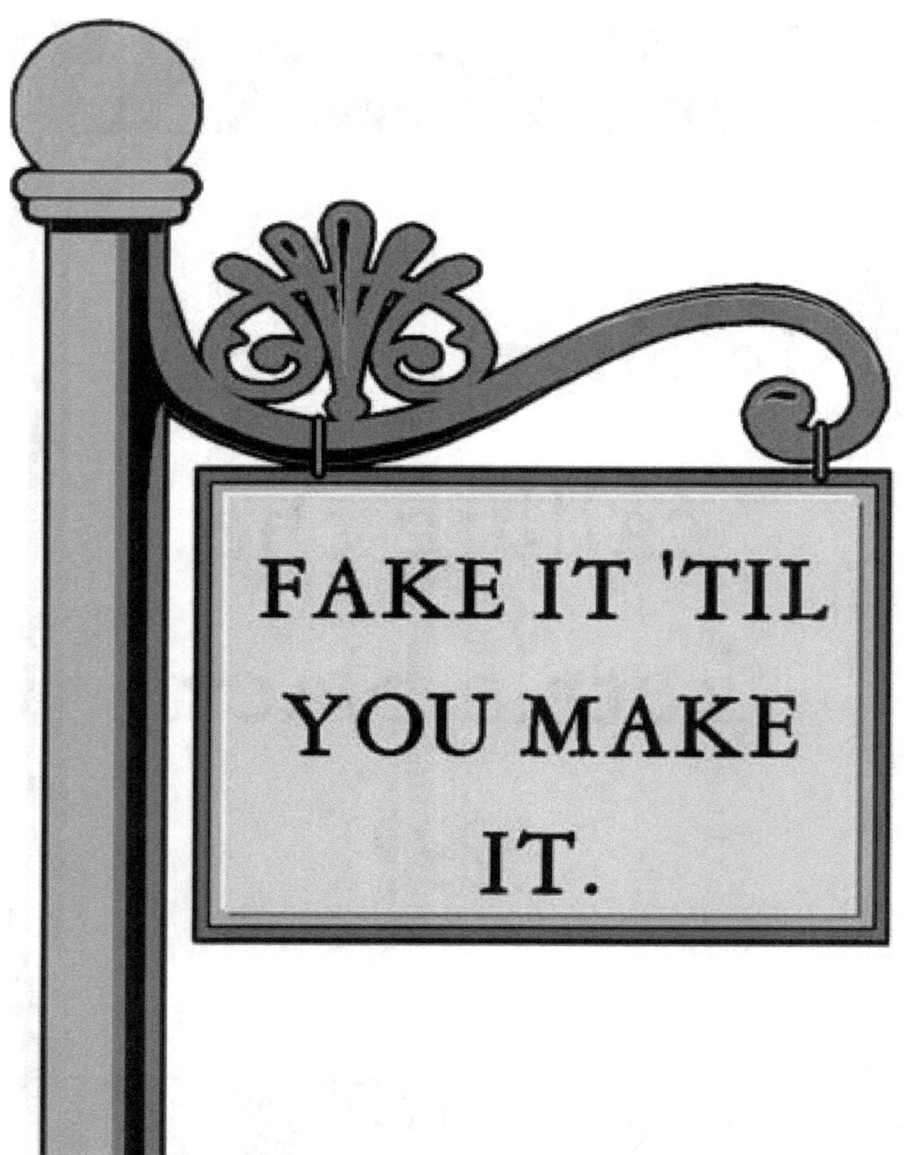
FAKE IT 'TIL
YOU MAKE
IT.

ABOUT THE AUTHOR

DeVita M. Ledgister, a World Language teacher at a prestigious charter school in South Philadelphia, was born on September 27, 1952 and raised in West Philadelphia, Pennsylvania. She has taught French, Spanish, Latin and/or German during her entire teaching career throughout Pennsylvania and neighboring states. Her father, Newton, was born of Jamaican parentage. Her mother, Delia, born in North Carolina was the first person of color to be hired by a major pharmaceutical company within the United States of America.

Although DeVita has presently settled down on the northeast coast, she has spent a lot of time living in various places throughout America. She completed her academic undergraduate years at Grambling University in the heart of Louisiana during the '70's, after which upon graduation, she relocated to the west coast area. She began her teaching career as a substitute teacher at a nearby high school in Bakersfield. Soon she relocated to Los Angeles as she developed an interest for business. She became a bank branch trainer while trying to fulfill a desire to complete her law school degree at the University of West Los Angeles Law School. Later, she returned to the Philadelphia area to attend LaSalle University and receive her Masters in Education.

During the end of the 1980's and the beginning of the 1990's, DeVita attended school in Cuernavaca, Modelos, Mexico for a time via the LaSalle University Emersion Program. She then secured not one, but three Fulbright Teacher Exchange Scholarships from Washington, D.C. to Wales, Canada and Senegal.

DeVita's interest in world languages was stimulated by her first high school Foreign Language teacher. As her academic life flourished, she became more interested in languages and how to communicate with others outside her own community and cultural circle. Her flare for writing also began in high school when her English teach explained to her "in order to become a writer you must write." Thus, years of writing journals, plays, poetry, short stories, screen plays and newspaper articles were born. She says her next writing endeavor is to have her two Spanish textbooks revised and published.

www.ingramcontent.com/pod-product-compliance
Lightning Source LLC
Chambersburg PA
CBHW070644120726
47909CB00004B/1571

* 9 7 8 0 9 8 4 3 2 5 5 4 2 *